Clifford THE BIG RED DOG®

THE STORMY DAY RESCUE

Adapted by Kimberly Weinberger

Illustrated by Del and Dana Thompson

**Based on the Scholastic book series
"Clifford The Big Red Dog"
by Norman Bridwell**

From the television script
"Stormy Weather" by Bruce Talkington and Dev Ross

SCHOLASTIC INC.

New York   Toronto   London   Auckland   Sydney   Mexico City
New Delhi   Hong Kong

No part of this publication may be reproduced, or stored in a retrieval system, or transmitted in any form or by any means, electronic, mechanical, photocopying, recording, or otherwise, without written permission of the publisher. For information regarding permission, write to Scholastic Inc., Attention: Permissions Department, 555 Broadway, New York, NY 10012.

ISBN 0-439-21360-6

Library of Congress Cataloging-in-Publication Data available

27   14/0

Printed in the U.S.A.   40
First printing, February 2001

One day, Clifford found

a very big bone.

"I will bury it," Clifford said.

Cleo and T-Bone helped

him find a good spot.

Not far away,

Samuel was serving lunch.

"It looks as if we might

get a storm," he said.

Just then, sand began to fly.

"I asked for a fish

sandwich," said Victor,

"not a *sand*

sandwich!"

Samuel looked down.

He saw Clifford digging.

"You are getting sand

in the food!" said Samuel.

Clifford was sorry.

"Please go dig somewhere

else," Samuel said.

Soon Clifford, Cleo, and
T-Bone found a better spot
for the bone.

"You don't even

have to dig," said T-Bone.

"The hole is already there."

But the hole

was not deep enough

for the bone.

Clifford dug deeper.

When he finished,

Mr. Howard came to the hole.

He dropped a tree inside.

It fell to the bottom.

"How did this hole

get so deep?"

asked Mr. Howard.

Clifford barked happily.

"That hole was for this tree!"

Mr. Howard said.

"Please go dig somewhere else."

Meanwhile, the storm
grew closer.
At the school,
Miss Carrington's class
was worried.

"Remember when the last storm flooded the library?" Jetta said. "Maybe it will happen again."

"Maybe the wind

will blow things around,"

said Charley. "Like that!"

The class looked outside.

Dirt was flying everywhere!

"Clifford!" called Emily Elizabeth.

"You can't dig a hole here,"

said Emily Elizabeth.

"We are having a class."

Clifford hung his head.

Emily Elizabeth patted Clifford's nose.

"You had better go home now,"

she said.

Clifford decided

to bury his bone

in his own backyard.

He said good-bye

to Cleo and T-Bone.

Next door,

Mr. and Mrs. Bleakman

worked in their garden.

The Bleakmans

were covering their flowers

to save them from

the storm.

Clifford began to dig.

Dirt flew into

the Bleakman's yard.

Poor Clifford was told

to dig somewhere else—again.

The storm was moving closer.

Everyone met at the library.

They began to build a wall of dirt.

It would keep the waves out

during the storm.

"We have to make the wall
very high," said Mr. Howard.
"That's a lot of digging!"
said Charley.

"I know the best digger around!"

cried Emily Elizabeth. "Clifford!"

"Dig, boy," Emily Elizabeth said.

But Clifford would not dig.

Clifford just sat.

Emily Elizabeth understood.

"All digging isn't bad," she said.

"It's just that there's a right time

and place for it."

Before long, the wall was built.

Clifford saved the library!

Later, everyone gave

Clifford bones

for his hard work.

"I'll help you bury them,"

Emily Elizabeth said.

"Somewhere perfect—just like you!"

Do You Remember?

Circle the right answer.

1. What did Clifford want to bury?
   a. a toy
   b. a bone
   c. a shoe

2. Everyone was afraid _____ would flood in the storm.
   a. the school
   b. Clifford's doghouse
   c. the library

Which happened first?
Which happened next?
Which happened last?
Write a 1, 2, or 3 in the space after each sentence.

Clifford dug in his own backyard. _____

Emily Elizabeth sent
Clifford home.   _____

Clifford helped build the wall.   _____

Answers:

Clifford helped build the wall. (3)
Emily Elizabeth sent Clifford home. (1)
Clifford dug in his own backyard. (2)
1-b; 2-c.